Lucky Luke's Hunting Adventures

The Swamp

Extended Version

by Kevin Lovegreen
with Illustrations by Nathan Boemer

Lucky Luke's Hunting Adventures: The Swamp Extended Version © 2012 by Kevin Lovegreen.
All rights reserved. No part of this book may be reproduced in any form whatsoever, by photography or xerography or by any other means, by broadcast or transmission, by translation into any kind of language, nor by recording electronically or otherwise, without permission in writing from the author, except by a reviewer, who may quote brief passages in critical articles or reviews.

Illustrated by Nathan Boemer

ISBN 13: 978-0-9857179-0-2

Printed in the United States of America

First Printing: 2012

16 15 14 13 12   5 4 3 2 1

Cover and interior design by James Monroe Design, LLC.

Lucky Luke, LLC.
4335 Matthew Drive
Eagan, Minnesota 55123
LuckyLukeHunting.com

Quantity discounts available!

*This book is dedicated to my dad for
introducing me to the
amazing world of hunting.
His love for the outdoors and his passion for
the hunt inspired me at a very young age to
follow in his footsteps.
I am forever grateful.*

Thanks Dad!

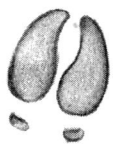

Chapter 1

"Please pass me another venison steak. As usual, it's mouth-watering perfect, Dad," I said.

"Enjoy it, because it's our last meal of venison. The freezer's empty," Dad replied.

"I sure am glad the rifle season opens next week," Crystal piped in. "Just like last November, I will have to show you boys up and shoot a nice deer to fill the freezer."

"You just wait, beginner's luck will help me shoot a monster buck!" I said with confidence.

"Luke, I can't believe you're finally old enough to be out there and show your dad how to get a big buck," Mom smiled.

"It's been a long wait, but I'm ready. I just hope a little of Crystal's luck rubs off on me."

"That's all you need, girl luck!" Vernon teased.

"I know you're ready, buddy," Dad said. "You have the passion and you've worked hard to prepare yourself. I just hope your guide can put you in the right spot."

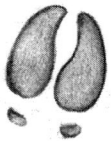

When you grow up in a hunting family you're introduced to the outdoors at an early age. I can't even remember the first time my dad took me walking in the woods, looking for deer sign. There is a picture of Dad and me up on the wall at my grandparents' cabin. I'm all bundled up in a baby backpack, and they say I loved to go along for the ride, when Dad went walking in the woods.

Both Vernon and Crystal have been lucky enough to join the hunters at grandma and grandpa's cabin in northern Minnesota for whitetail deer. Grandpa's rule is that you have to be twelve years old to participate in the opening weekend of the season, which we just call the opener.

Over the last two seasons, Crystal has been really lucky and outdone Dad and Vernon. She kids that it's all skill, but

Vernon, and I know that Dad has a bunch to do with it. Dad and Crystal sat in some great spots over the last two seasons and Crystal has managed to shoot two nice does. For a girl, Crystal sure knows how to handle a gun, and she should: Dad has been encouraging her—and all of us kids—to shoot since we were little.

Crystal loves to hunt, but when it comes to shooting guns, Vernon and I can't seem to get enough. I was seven years old when I got my first BB gun. It was my birthday, and it was one of the best birthdays ever. My whole family came to celebrate: Vernon, Crystal, and all my cousins surrounded me when I opened up my BB gun. I couldn't wait to get to the cabin to try it out with dad.

Dad is always talking to us kids about gun safety. Before I even held a gun, I knew a bunch of the rules. Things like, everyone has to stay behind the shooter. You have to know what's beyond your target. You always have to keep your barrel pointed in a safe direction (down at the ground, or up at the sky). And most importantly, you always, always make sure your safety is on.

Ever since I took that first shot with my BB gun, my brother and I have been putting holes in targets, cans, and as many squirrels as we can find at my grandparents' cabin. Vernon is three years older than me, so that gave him a head start on shooting. But that just made me practice more and try harder to be as good of a shot as him. At this point, I think I can hold my own with Vernon and Crystal both.

As all of us kids got bigger, Dad introduced us to bigger guns. After starting with BB guns, we moved on to pellet guns, a

.22 rifle, a 410 shotgun, a 20-gauge shotgun, a 12-gauge shotgun, a .44 Magnum rifle, and a .243 rifle. The BB gun, pellet gun, and .22 rifle are great guns for shooting targets and squirrels. They shoot a single round and take lots of practice to become a good shot. The .44 Magnum and .243 rifle are great for hunting deer. They are powerful enough for a clean kill on a deer but not too powerful for us kids to handle.

Shotguns, like the 410, 20-, and 12-gauge, are great for shooting clay targets and game birds. They shoot out a bunch of small BBs and have a big pattern (that means the BBs spread out a lot), so you have a better chance at hitting a flying bird. We are really lucky to have the opportunity to use all these different guns.

When I was nine, Dad let me carry a single-shot 410 shotgun as we walked the woods and fields looking for grouse. I only carried one shell, in my hand, and if it was my turn and there was enough time, I could load the gun and walk in front of Dad, Vernon, and Crystal and then, if it was still there, try to shoot the grouse. It took me a long time to get my first bird, but I always loved going along and trying.

One thing for sure, by the time I was ten, there wasn't anywhere around the cabin that was a safe place for a squirrel. Grandpa had us on patrol for squirrels, the red ones in particular. He wanted us to keep them away from the cabin because they chewed their way into the attic one year and made a big mess. The best thing about squirrels, especially the big grey ones, is that they are great eating. Grandma always told me, you shoot and clean them, I will cook them. That deal was good for squirrel, grouse, rabbit, and fish. I think she's the best cook in the world!

When I was ten years old Dad got me my first wild turkey license and he took me out that spring. We had a great time and I still think a tom turkey gobble is one of the coolest sounds an animal can make. We hunted really hard and I learned a lot that weekend, and I finally got a chance at my first turkey. That's an adventure I won't forget!

Chapter 2

In the summers, Dad, Vernon, and I go out in the woods and scout for deer. Dad loves to follow deer runways and see where they cross each other. He's always trying to find the perfect spot for a deer stand. He watches from back in the woods while Vernon and I walk down the runways and he figures out what tree would have the best shot if we were deer. The fun really begins when we get the nails and hammers out and start building deer stands. Dad does all the cutting and hammering. Vernon and I hand him the wood and help him hold the pieces in place. When we all work together, we can build a stand in about an hour.

Early in the archery deer hunting season, Dad takes me out with him. I love to sit and watch him try to get a deer. The time flies when we see deer and have a lot of action. I will never forget the evening we were sitting in the old deer stand off the clover field. Like a ghost, a nice eight-point buck appeared from the thick woods and began walking right to us. Dad raised his bow and drew back the arrow. I didn't move a muscle; I had my eyes locked on the buck. At just the right time, Dad made a grunt sound and the buck stopped in its tracks. Right then, Dad let his arrow fly and hit the buck perfect. That was one of the coolest things I have ever seen. I can't wait until I get my chance at a buck like that one.

Hunting isn't always exciting. The times that we don't see anything moving, well, that tends to get a little tiring. That's when I lay my head on Dad's shoulder and take a nap. Dad says, "I'll stand guard while you take ten." Sometimes I think I go a little longer than ten minutes, but Dad never complains. One time I was taking ten and Dad nudged me. I woke up and looked down and there were a doe and fawn eating right below our stand. That was a great way to wake up.

When I was almost twelve, I was old enough to take gun safety classes offered by the Department of Natural Resources. The classes taught me a bunch of stuff about hunting and gun safety. A lot of it was stuff my dad, grandpa, and uncles had taught me as I grew up in a family that loved hunting. But there were also new things that I learned. The classes really helped me become a safe, well-rounded outdoorsman. I was really proud when I passed my test and received my Firearm Safety Certificate. A great thing about earning my certificate is that it permits me to buy any hunting license offered in Minnesota, and I can't wait to try them all!

Chapter 3

It had been a long week since we ate the last of our venison, but now the sun was going down on Friday night before the opener as Dad, Vernon, Crystal, and I pulled up to my grandma and grandpa's cabin. We walked in and were greeted by Grandpa, Uncle Jim, and our cousins John, Steve, and Justin.

"Welcome to the North Country!" Grandpa howled.

"The grill's on. We're just waiting for the chef," Uncle Jim said to my dad. Everyone pitched in unpacking the truck as Dad worked the grill like a pro.

The smell of Dad's mouth-watering hamburgers filled the cabin as we sat down to eat. Grandpa laughed. "Burgers and baked beans! Your grandma would have a heart attack if she knew that's all we had. At deer camp, we keep things simple," he said with a smile.

After dinner, everyone began their preparations for the morning hunt. I watched Uncle Jim open a bottle of deer scent and put it on cotton pads. He was very careful not to get any on his fingers. "Take a whiff!" Uncle Jim dared me. I did, and when I just about threw up, I quickly understood why he was being careful not to get it on his fingers. "That's my trick to getting the bucks to stop by my stand. I carry the cotton pads out in a Ziploc bag and hang them on the trees around my stand. Bucks can't resist this stuff!" Uncle Jim said, with not a hint of doubt in his voice.

Vernon was putting deer scent on a rag. "What are you going to do with that?" I asked.

"I'm going to drag it from my boot on the way to my stand. I read an article in a hunting magazine, and they swear by it. I'm going to have the deer lining up at my stand in the morning. You just watch and see," he said.

Crystal, who was lucky enough to be at her third opener, showed Grandpa how she rattled antlers to attract deer. She made it sound just like two bucks fighting. "That will get a big buck running to join the fight," she told me with confidence.

"Hey Dad, what's your trick?" I asked.

As usual, he answered with very few words. "I sit still and be quiet," he said. "If you're moving, they usually see you before you see them."

That made sense to me because I remembered sitting with my grandpa early one morning at the cabin. A deer appeared out of the thick woods, and cautiously eased up to the bird feeder. I remember my grandpa telling me that deer can see the slightest movement and hear the smallest sound. "Don't move a muscle and let's see if she eats the birdseed," Grandpa said. As she was walking up, I reached over for my hot cocoa, and in a flash, she took off. I remember Grandpa looking at me and saying, "Didn't I tell you not to move a muscle?" Well, I guess he wasn't kidding—those deer sure can see movement. I told him I was sorry, but I remember really wanting a sip of that hot cocoa.

It sure was fun listening to all the strategies that everyone was going to try. I couldn't wait to get out in the woods and see which one works for me!

After a while, Dad stood up and said, "OK, it's time to get all your stuff laid out! We don't want any hold-ups in the morning." Like rockets, Vernon, Crystal, and I headed to our duffel bags and made sure our gear was ready.

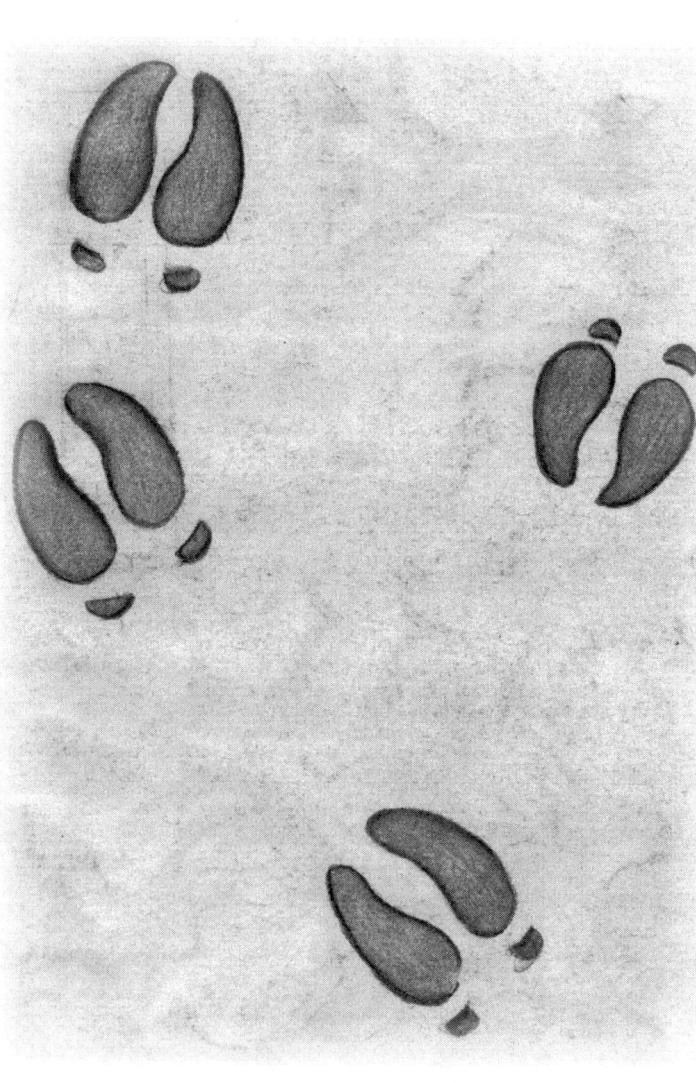

Chapter 4

It wasn't long until everyone made their way back to the living room, to share stories of past openers. "Remember the time that big buck stood in the field and Grandpa pulled up his gun three times trying to see it through his scope?" said Uncle Jim. "And when he realized the scope was filled with snow, he was so mad, he just about threw his gun at the buck!"

"What about the time Dad shot that big buck way back in the swamp? It took us three hours to drag it out! I swear it weighed three hundred pounds!" Vernon piped in.

There were so many fun stories to share, and I couldn't wait to be a part of them. Then Crystal asked, "Grandpa, where are you going in the morning?" That started a whole new discussion as everyone debated where to go.

My grandpa looked at me and smiled. "This is your first deer camp, Luke, so you don't understand how important this question is. You want to pick a deer stand that is right for the wind. If the wind is blowing in the direction the deer are coming from, they will smell you and they're gone. You'll never even see them," Grandpa said with a knowing wink.

I was impressed. My grandpa sure knew a lot about deer hunting—and he should, he's been doing it f-o-r-e-v-e-r.

"Quiet! The weather is on the radio!" Grandpa shouted. Instantly, everyone went silent and listened to the announcer.

"For your deer opener, it's going to be a northwest wind at ten to twelve miles per hour and a cool twenty-eight degrees, warming to thirty-five."

Grandpa turned to me and winked. "Now we know what stand to choose and how warm to dress."

"That's not going to work for my lucky stand by Boney's Lake. Now where should I go?" Uncle Jim moaned.

It was at that moment I realized my dad hadn't said where we would be going. Maybe he wanted to keep it a secret, but I had to ask. "Dad, where are we going in the morning?"

He slowly looked at me and said nothing for a moment, before he answered. "The swamp. That's where I always go opening morning. Big bucks live in the swamp. I hope you're up to the walk. It's a long way out there."

I had a big smile on my face, picturing this magical place with giant deer. "You bet!" I said bravely.

Dad continued. "You better dress warm, it's going to be cold out there. And remember, we have to wear hip boots on the way out because the water is deep."

"Water?" I asked, confused.

"Yes, water." Dad confirmed.

Vernon looked at me with a smirk on his face. "I got to go last year with Dad, and it's a long, hard walk, but it's worth it. I didn't see any deer last year, but I know they're out there. You have to walk forever on this wet, swampy bog stuff, and then you come to an island in the middle of the swamp. Last year Dad dropped me off at a deer stand and told me not to leave."

"Why did Dad tell you not to leave?" I asked.

"Because as soon as you move—BAM! The deer sees you before you see it. When I was sitting there silently in that deer stand, I heard this huge buck coming through the woods! Well, I think it was a huge buck. I never saw it, but I could hear the antlers clicking on the branches as it walked. The buck was just out of my sight. If I could have snuck out of the stand and walked closer to it, I would have seen it. But Dad said to stay in the stand, and that was okay with me. I'd heard wolves howling earlier and I knew they were out there somewhere.

I believe that big buck is still there, and I'm going to get him tomorrow morning!" my brother said with confidence.

"Okay kids, enough stories. It's time for bed. Morning is going to come quick," Dad said.

We jumped up and headed to our sleeping bags.

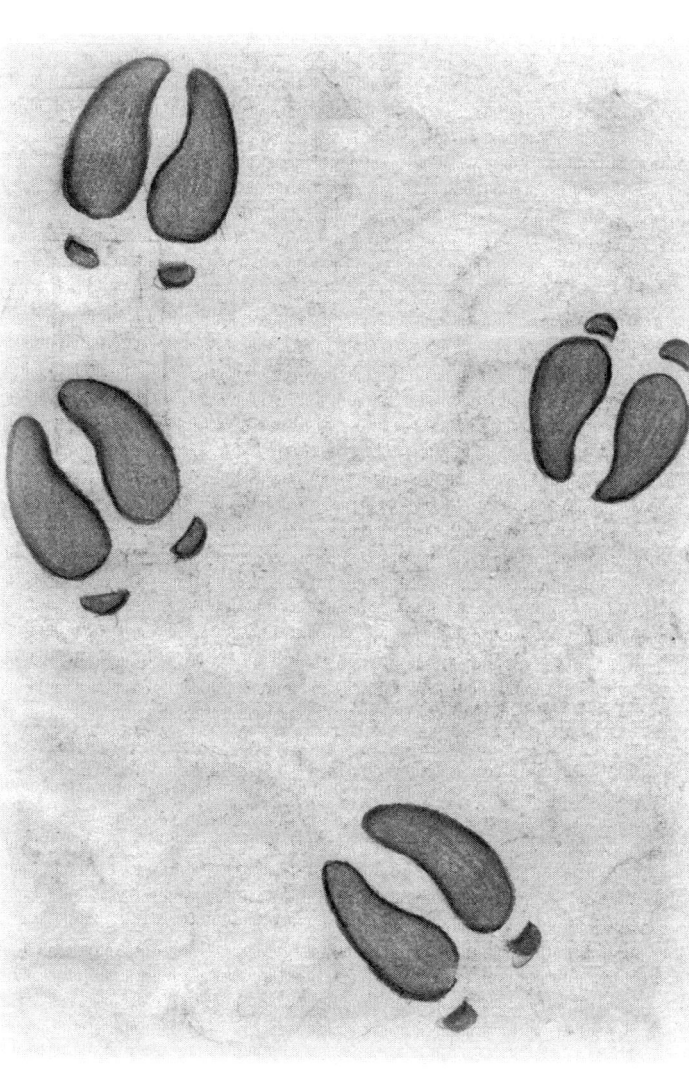

Chapter 5

It seemed like I had just closed my eyes when I was jolted awake by a loud banging and my Uncle Jim singing. I couldn't believe my eyes—or my ears. "It's a beautiful morning, it's a beautiful day, all the birds are chirping, and everything's going my way!" my uncle sang. He kept singing and banging on a pan with a wooden spoon until everyone was up. "If I'm up, everyone should be up!" he bellowed in his long underwear.

I popped out of bed and got dressed. After a quick bowl of cereal, I went back to my gear to make sure I had everything Dad had told me to bring. I pulled on my heavy wool socks and a big orange jacket. I had my bullets (three for my gun and three for backup, just like Dad told me), my little flashlight, a compass, a few sticks of beef jerky, a bottle of water, and two small Snickers bars that Grandpa had given me. I was ready!

Before anyone else had their jackets on, Dad, Vernon, Crystal, and I were out the door. "We have the farthest to go, so we need to get going early," Dad said.

We walked outside. It was dark, cold, and quiet. The doors to the old green Jeep creaked as we opened them and climbed in. Dad started the engine, and we headed down the driveway and turned onto the old dirt road.

My eyes started to get heavy listening to the rumble of the Jeep on the long, bumpy ride. I sparked back up when we slowed down and pulled over next to a little clearing. Dad turned off the ignition but kept the lights on. In the yellow glow, we pulled our hip boots on. We tied the laces of our hunting boots together and slung them over our shoulders. Once we were ready, Dad cut the Jeep's lights, and off we went into the darkness, pushing deeper toward the swamp.

It was cold and mysterious walking with the full moon shining through the thick pine trees. You couldn't hear anything except our boots crunching on the frozen ground.

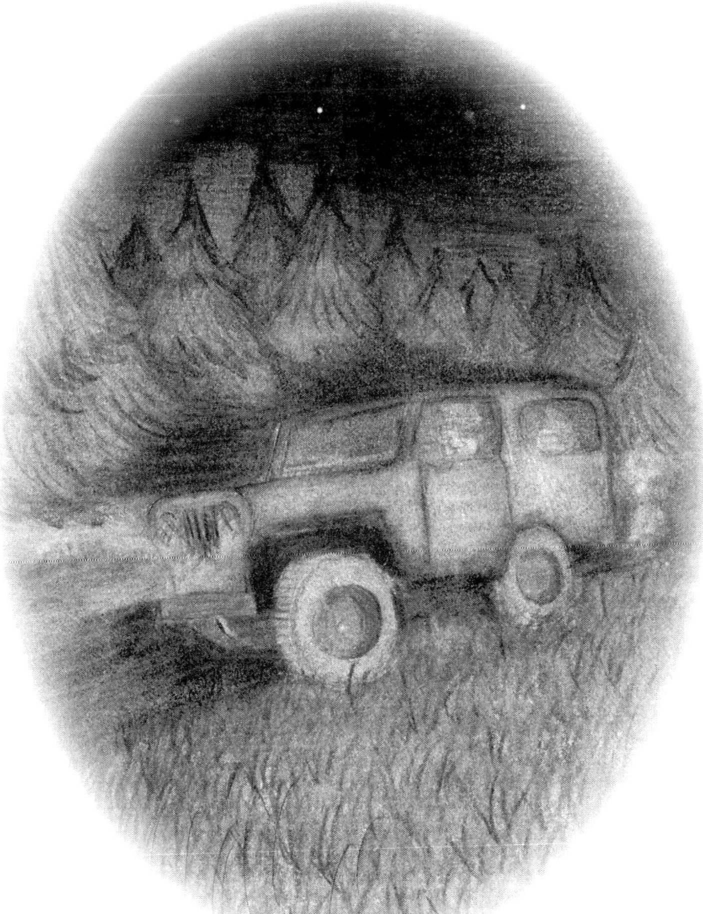

Dad led the way, Crystal second, Vernon third, and me in back. After a long march, we arrived at a wooden deer stand on the edge of the trail.

"This is your stand, Crystal," Dad said.

"It sure is. Good luck in the swamp, boys. Push a big buck my way if you can. It will be a lot less dragging if I get one out here," Crystal joked. Dad watched Crystal climb carefully up the wooden ladder and into the stand. He slid her gun up to her and she gave us a thumbs up.

We walked a little farther and came to a trail that looked like it was cut right out of the darkness. "Be careful, and try not to fall," Dad said. We started trekking through the swamp. It was tough walking, and my feet seemed to stick deeper in the mud with every step. Each time I pulled my foot out, it made a funny slurping sound, and Vernon and I laughed. Even with the laughter, it was a little bit scary out in the swamp in the dark. I felt safer being close to Vernon and Dad, and didn't want to fall behind, so I did everything I could to keep up.

Finally, we came to a spot where the ground was hard again. "We made it. This is the island," my dad said quietly. We took off our hip boots and put on our regular boots. They were freezing cold from the walk. I was hoping my feet would warm them up quick, but it took a while, even with more hiking.

It was still dark, and I felt like we had been walking for hours. The anticipation was killing me. I wanted to get to our spot, but I didn't know where it was, so I had no idea if we were close or still far away.

We started walking down an old trail that seemed like it had been there for a long time, because the trees alongside it towered above us. I started wondering why someone would cut a trail in the middle of a swamp. I pictured an old trapper wrapped in furs, walking his mule down the trail with a load of traps and a bundle of animal hides. Maybe my boots were stepping in his tracks.

It wasn't long before we reached another wooden deer stand just off the trail. "Good luck guys," Vernon said, and without hesitation, he shot up the ladder and sat down on a little chair.

"Let's go," Dad whispered, and our journey continued.

We reached a turn in the trail with a bunch of long logs stacked up on one side. "This is our spot," Dad said. "You sit on that side of the log pile and keep watch down the trail. I will sit on this side. You can load your gun just like we practiced this summer."

Well, this is it, I thought to myself. With my little flashlight in my mouth, I pulled my .44 Magnum bullets out of my pocket. The bullets were cold, and I was careful not to drop them. I made sure my gun's safety was on. Then I pushed the bullets into the bottom of the gun, just like Dad had taught me, and with a click of the action, the gun was loaded. I was hunting!

I found a sneaky spot in the log pile where I could squeeze in and feel like I was hidden if a deer came by. My heart was pounding and my hands were sweating. I took my gloves off to let the heat out and took a couple slow deep breaths to calm down.

As I noticed and absorbed the silence, I began to hear things that I had never heard before. I felt like I could hear steam coming from my jacket. With every breath I took, my jacket moved up and down, and I could hear the soft orange fabric make a sliding sound. I could even hear myself swallow, and it sounded loud.

I practiced slowly raising my gun, as if a deer was coming, to see if I could do it without making any noise. I heard myself move every time—this was going to be hard! My dad and grandpa told me the deer can hear any noise you make. I figured I would have to keep a close watch so I would see a deer coming from a long way off and get ready. That was my plan.

As the dawn light began to fill the woods, I watched like a hawk, scanning the forest for a deer. That lasted about ten minutes, though it seemed like an hour. Then I heard something move behind me. My heart froze, and the thoughts in my head evaporated. I stopped breathing, so I wouldn't make any noise, and slowly turned to see what was there. Suddenly I saw a small black flash and heard a little crackling sound, and I realized what made the noise. It was a mouse!

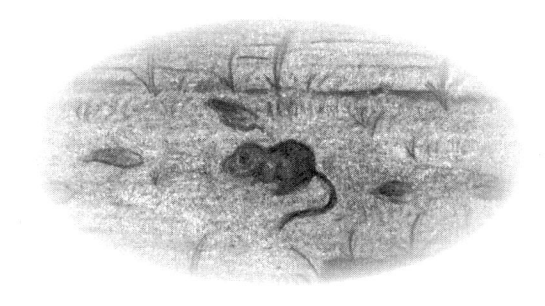

I let out a long stream of air as if I had been holding my breath for two minutes. Maybe I had! As the heat that had overtaken my body started to cool down, I thought to myself, *If a mouse makes that much noise, I can't imagine how loud a deer will be.* That's when I realized how much you can hear in the woods when you are sitting perfectly still. I was suddenly aware of all kinds of things I had never noticed before. There were crows off in the distance. Up until then, I had never really listened to a crow. I figured they made one call, and it was caw, caw, caw.

Now I was listening to this crazy new language of noises they were making. Each sound was so distinct it was easy to believe they were talking.

At that moment, a little chickadee landed on the small branch a couple of feet from me and my heart fluttered again. Suddenly, a whole flock landed, and they were popping around the ground, the tree, and the twigs. It was cool watching them search for food, like I was getting to see a secret meeting. I felt like I was part of the log pile because the mouse, the crows, and the birds didn't seem to notice I was there.

Then I froze for a moment and thought, *Oops!* I hadn't even looked around to see if any deer were coming. I slowly scanned the area in front of me—NOTHING! This spot seemed like a great place to see deer, but then I got curious. What if a deer was standing just out of our sight? What if I couldn't see it and Dad couldn't see it, either? It was driving me crazy—I had to explore.

Chapter 6

I slowly slid out of the log pile. When my first step made a loud crunch from under my boot, I felt like I had just blown my cover. I froze, and Dad peeked around the log pile with a surprised look on his face. I slowly took the next step and tried as hard as I could not to make any noise. I walked like a tightrope walker, one step carefully and slowly in front of the other over to Dad.

"Can we go see if there is a better spot down the trail?" I asked.

"We've only been here thirty minutes," Dad whispered.

"I know, but I really want to see what's around the corner," I pleaded.

"OK, buddy, I'll let you pick out the next spot, but this has always been a great place to see deer," Dad said, shaking his head.

As we made our way down the trail, I felt that at any moment a deer would be standing in the next clearing. As we reached the corner, like it was a dream, I saw a flash far behind us. I looked quickly to see what it was, and like a ghost, there was a deer gliding through the trees right next to the log pile. And it wasn't just any deer—it was the biggest buck I had ever seen!

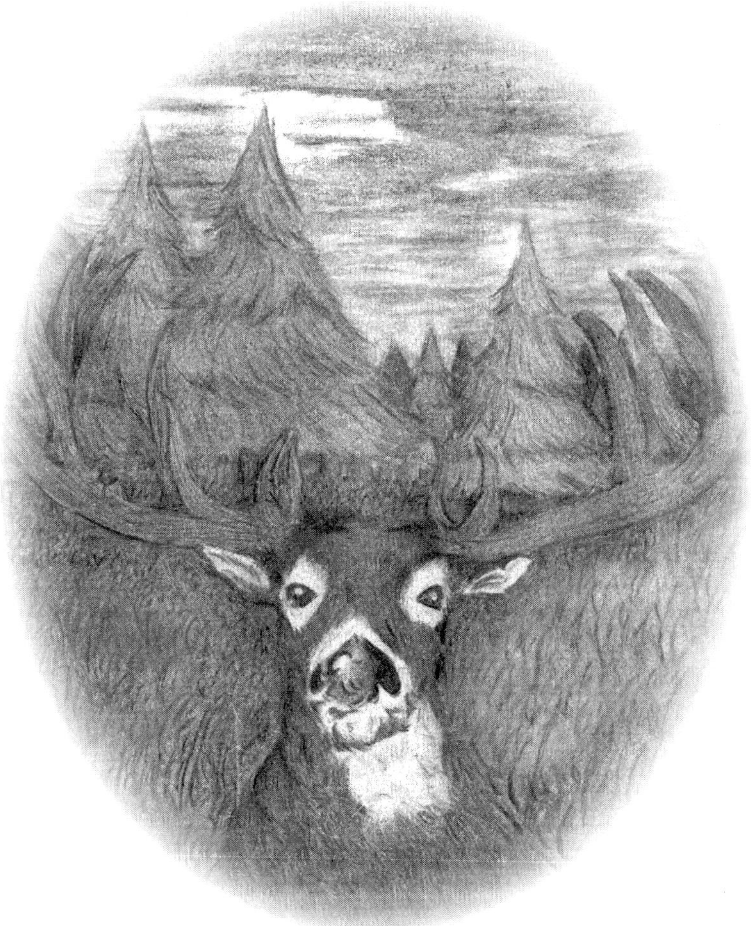

Dad also saw it and like the speed of light we pulled our guns up to shoot—but in that instant, the buck was gone. What really struck me was that it wasn't making a sound. How could this be? The mouse made noise, the little chickadees made noise, I made a bunch of noise, but this buck seemed to fly through the woods as though he were made of vapor.

I tried to get my wits back as I carefully scanned the area. Then I realized my mistake. If I would have stayed in one spot, like Dad suggested, that deer would not have seen us moving.

"Can you believe that?" Dad shook his head in amazement. "That buck was huge!"

"It was amazing! I can't believe it disappeared so quickly," I replied. "I guess we should have stuck it out a little longer at the log pile."

"That's one thing about hunting: you never know when the animals are going to show up. Patience usually pays off, and it's experiences like this that will help you stay in your spot a little longer next time." I could tell from how he said it, that he'd been there before.

Frustrated but needing a new plan, I encouraged Dad to keep sneaking a little farther down the trail to find a place to sit. As we came around another bend I saw a perfect little opening in the middle of the thick woods. There was a giant pine tree right in the middle of the opening, and it was calling my name.

"What do you think about sitting by that tree?" I pointed across the clearing.

"Looks good to me, let's give it a try," Dad whispered.

We quietly snuck up to the tree and sat down.

When I made myself perfectly still, the woods slowly began coming alive like before. I listened to a flock of geese from a distance, and as they got closer and closer their honking became louder and louder. I watched them fly over the trees in a perfect V shape.

My heart jumped as I heard an alarming CUK... CUK... CUK coming from across the clearing. It sounded like a bird, but it was so loud and sounded so strange, I couldn't think of what kind of bird it might be. As it flew closer, I saw that it was a huge pileated woodpecker with a bright red head. Realizing I was being distracted, I reminded myself, *Stay focused on deer, forget about the bird.*

Startling me, I heard a soft crunching sound to my left. I turned my head, and there it was—the giant buck stood about thirty yards away! I raised my gun, and luckily he didn't see me move!

"Take him," I heard Dad whisper from the other side of the tree.

In one motion, I clicked the safety off, put the open sight on his chest and pulled the trigger. BANG! The gun boomed.

The deer jumped back and then just stood there. I couldn't believe my eyes—he was supposed to fall over just like he had in my dreams. I quickly fired again, and this time the buck turned and bolted. I

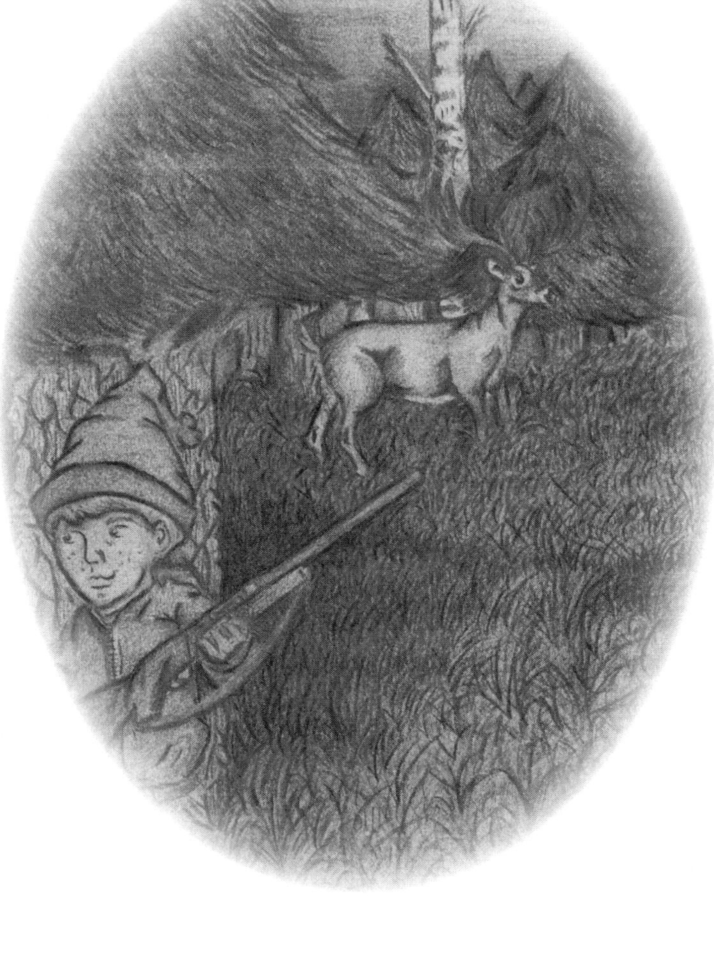

pulled the trigger once more, missing him as he ran. Then it was quiet again, except for the ringing in my ears and my heart pounding.

I sat in amazement. What had just happened? I couldn't have missed! How did he get there? How long was he standing there before I heard him? Why was I looking at that bird?

I ran over to where he had stood only a moment earlier, hoping I would find a sign that I'd hit him. There on the ground was a big clump of deer hair. No blood, just hair. "NO!" I yelled, kicking the ground.

Dad walked over with a somber look on his face and asked, "Well, any blood?" That was all it took.

Adrenaline and my emotions overtook me as I tried to understand what had just taken place, tears streaming down my face. "He was huge, he was huge!" was all I could say.

Dad wrapped his strong arms around me and held me tight. "It's all right. Just relax," he soothed. "We will take our time and look for blood." After a few deep breaths, I pointed to the ground where the hair was. "You can't get much closer than that," Dad smiled.

After Dad showed me what the buck's tracks looked like, it was easy to see where his hooves had torn up the ground as he ran. We followed the tracks for a while, but didn't find any blood. It was a clean miss. Several clean misses, in fact. I was heartbroken.

"Luke, it's okay. You missed your first deer. It was a clean miss, and that happens to the best of us," Dad said. "You'll have many more chances in your life to get a deer." Somehow it didn't seem to matter to me that I would get more chances. I had missed my first good chance at a monster buck, and that was hard to take.

"Now maybe someone else will get a chance at that big buck," Dad said, trying to make me feel better. Just then we heard a shot off in the distance. It was hard to tell what direction it came from, because the sound echoed through the woods. "We better go see who that was!" Dad said, raising his eyebrows.

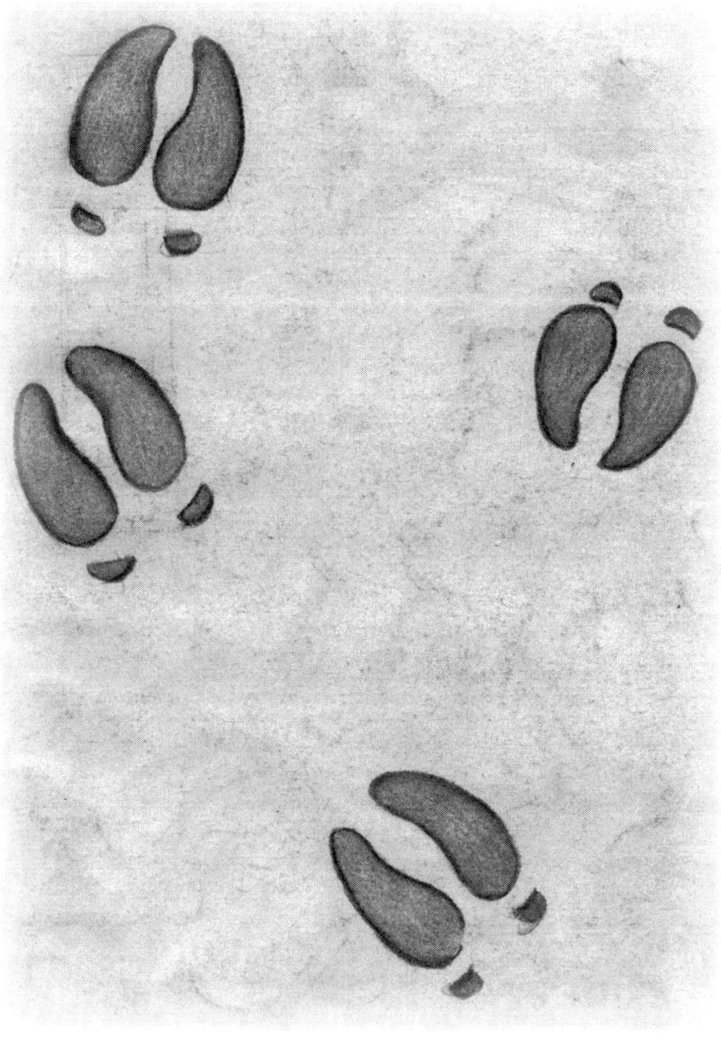

Chapter 7

We walked back down the trail and eventually came to Vernon sitting in his deer stand. "Did you shoot?" Dad asked.

"Not me," Vernon said. He quickly climbed down from the stand, anxious to talk to us. "I could hear shooting, Luke was it you? Did you get one?" Vernon asked with excitement.

"I missed a giant buck. I mean it was giant! He walked right up to me, and I didn't realize he was standing there. I skimmed him and took a pile of hair off his chest. I can't believe I missed him!"

"That's a bummer!" Vernon replied. "What about you, Dad, why didn't you get him?"

"He was on the other side of the tree from me, so I had no shot, but I got to see him. He was a beauty!"

As we made the long walk out of the swamp, I told the story a hundred times. I tried to explain to Vernon, over and over again, how big the buck was. I don't think he really believed the buck was as big as I kept telling him. When it came to telling stories, he knew I had a tendency to exaggerate a little. Every once in a while, Dad would simply add, "It was a big one."

We finally made it out and back to Crystal. She must have seen us coming, because she was already climbing down the ladder as we walked up. "I did it, I did it! I shot a giant buck!" Crystal squealed. She reached the ground and laid her gun down. Then she ran to Dad with her arms stretched high, jumping into him and just about knocking him over.

"Whoa! Good for you, Crystal!" Dad said, trying to keep his balance. "Where is he?"

"He ran that direction and disappeared." Crystal pointed into the woods.

"When did you shoot?" Dad asked.

"About forty-five minutes ago. I was too scared to go look for it without you," Crystal said to Dad.

"Well, do you think you made a good shot?" Dad asked.

"I think it was perfect. He ran out of the swamp and stopped over by that tree. I put the crosshairs of my scope right behind the shoulder and squeezed the trigger, just like I did on the doe I shot last year."

"Forty-five minutes should be long enough to let him lay. Let's go see if we can find some sign," Dad said.

We followed Dad to where Crystal said the deer was standing when she shot. It didn't take Dad long to find blood. "Looks like you hit him good." Dad said.

"I told you, I think it was a perfect shot." Crystal said. The red blood was easy to see on the fallen leaves.

We followed Dad as he weaved his way through the woods, keeping a close eye on the trail. It wasn't long before Dad said, "Take a look at that!" We all looked up, and there it was. A giant rack of antlers sticking out of the tall grass.

We all ran for the deer, excited to get a closer look. "Holy cow! That's the biggest deer I have ever seen!" Vernon shouted. Crystal and Dad knelt down next to the giant buck.

Crystal took her gloves off and ran her fingers through his thick hair. She patted his side and ran her hands over the massive antlers. "Oh my goodness, he is beautiful," Crystal said in awed disbelief.

Dad started counting the points out loud. When he got to sixteen, his voice started to get louder, as if he couldn't believe what he was saying. "Seventeen, eighteen, nineteen, twenty! You shot a twenty-point buck, Crystal!" Dad beamed. I didn't remember Dad ever getting this excited. We all hugged Crystal, jumping up and down in celebration. With that, Dad suddenly stopped and turned his head toward me. "Do you think this is the same buck that you missed back in the swamp?"

"I don't know. This buck seems a lot bigger than the one I shot at." Then my eyes got huge as a thought came bursting into my head. "What about the hair?" I wondered aloud.

We all turned and looked at the buck. The way he was laying, we couldn't see his chest. Dad heaved with all his might and lifted the buck's head up higher. To our surprise, there on his chest was a bare spot, where a big clump of hair was missing.

With renewed confidence, I looked at Vernon. "I told you it was huge! Now do you believe me?"

"He looks bigger than I remember him back in the swamp," Dad said.

"Nice haircut you gave him!" Vernon joked.

"Thanks for missing him for me, buddy!" Crystal teased.

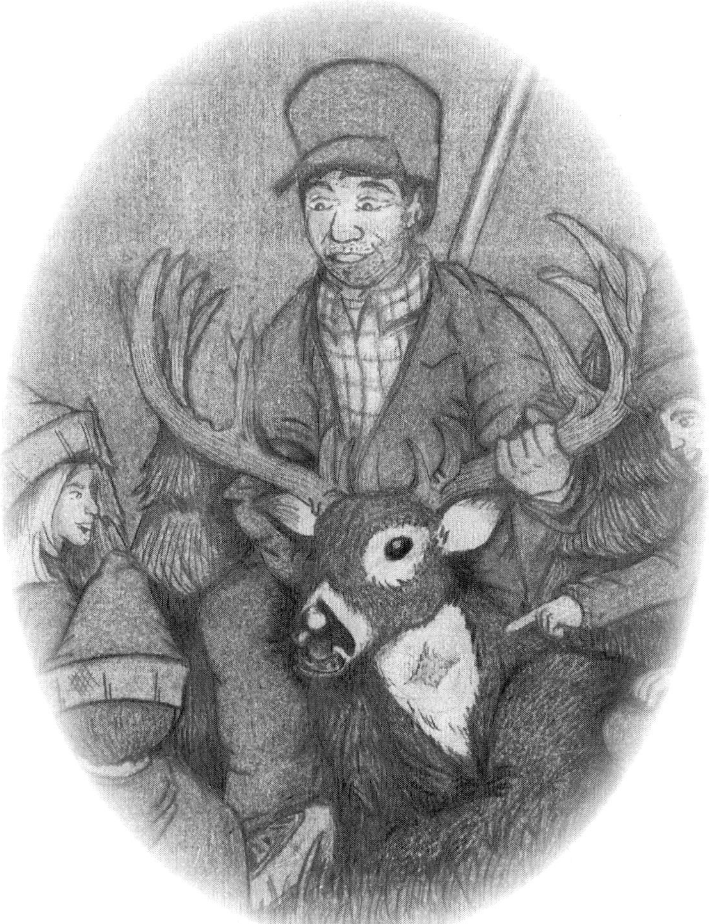

"Luke," Dad said, "I know it's not going to make you feel much better, but Crystal has been hunting longer than you have. She has done a lot of practice shooting and put in a great deal of time in the woods. Hopefully, one day, you will get another chance at a deer like this. You should be proud of your sister for making a great shot, and you should be really proud of yourself for almost getting a deer like this on your first hunting trip."

"I am proud of her," I answered. "If someone else had to get him, I'm glad it was her. She's a great hunter. And we all know if Vernon had shot a buck like this, we would never hear the end of it." We all laughed except Vernon; he didn't think that was funny.

"Let's take some pictures and get this beauty back to the cabin. Everyone is going to want to see this deer." Dad said, bursting with pride.

Dad was right—everyone was amazed by the deer and Crystal was a hero. Grandpa was so proud of Crystal, for dinner, he let her sit at the head of the table, his sacred spot. After dinner, we continued sharing our hunting stories of the day, but it wasn't long before the excitement and effort caught up to us. It was time for bed. As I closed my eyes and thought about everything that had happened that magical day, it made me realize one thing for certain—I was hooked on deer hunting. It was one of the greatest days of my life.

About the author

Kevin Lovegreen was born, raised, and lives in Minnesota with his loving wife and two amazing children. Hunting, fishing, and the outdoors have always been a big part of his life. From chasing squirrels as a child to chasing elk as an adult, Kevin loves the thrill of hunting, but even more, he loves telling the stories of the adventure. Presenting at schools and connecting with kids about the outdoors, is one of his favorite things to do.

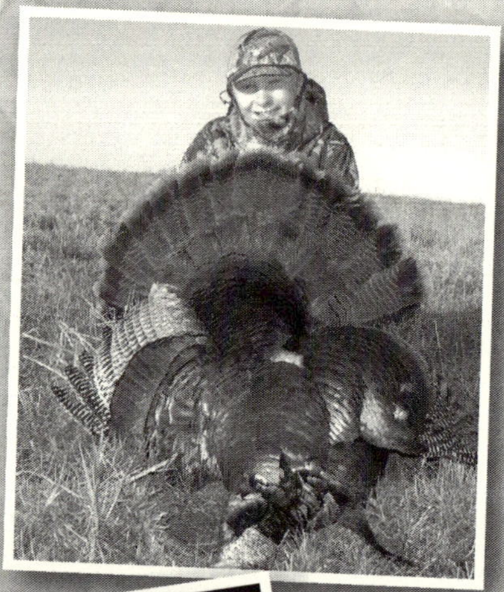
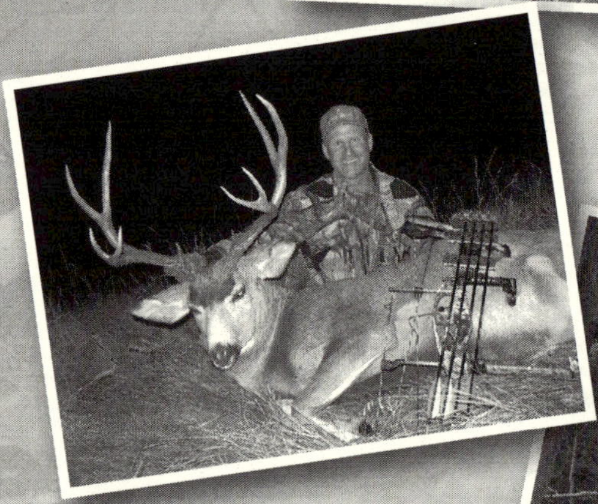
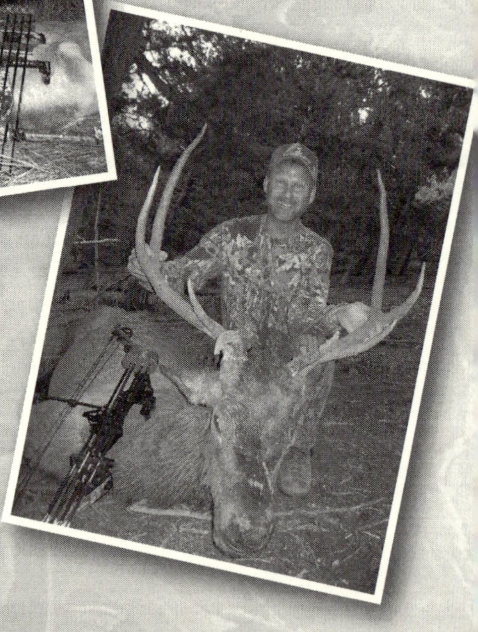

MORE! LUCKY LUKE'S HUNTING ADVENTURES

Turkey Tales
Winner, Winner, Turkey Dinner
Monster Mule Deer
The Muddy Elk

To order the
Lucky Luke's Hunting Adventures Series
visit: **LuckyLukeHunting.com**